TEDDY
and The Fire Brigade

One morning in the autumn when leaves start to fall,
Teddy was outside his house, kicking a ball.
"I've nothing special to do," he sighed.
"I can't think of a thing, and I've really tried."

"Can you gather some logs for me?" asked Mrs Bear.
"Then I'll light a fire, there's a chill in the air!"
"Right away!" called Teddy and kicked his ball high.
'There's a pile near the shed that I know are quite dry.

"May my friends come to lunch?" Teddy asked with a smile.
"If I give them a call, they'll be round in a while."
"I'll cook sausages and beans!" laughed Mrs Bear.
"That's what they ask for each time they come here."

Mrs Bear struck a match to make the logs light,
  But the thick clouds of smoke gave her a fright.
"Our chimney must be on fire! Help!" Teddy cried.
  "Leave the room. Close the door. We must both
  wait outside!"

"Send for the fire brigade, I'll make the call,"
   Just inside the backdoor was a 'phone on the wall.
Smoke poured from the house and swirled around,
   Teddy hugged Mrs Bear, "We're both safe and sound."

Just then Teddy's friends rushed out of the wood.
   "We smelled smoke and got here as quick as we could!"
Suddenly the fire engine came flying past,
   "Hurrah!" Teddy cheered, "you got here fast."

Leading Fireman Bear was the one to decide,
That masks must be worn to venture inside.
The smoke was so thick it was quite hard to see.
"There's no fire here, it's a real mystery!
We've found plenty of smoke, but no fire at all.
Did you see any flames when you gave us a call?"

"I've just had an idea!" said Fireman Bear.
"Let's get down the ladders and see what's up there!"
He climbed to the top of the chimney so tall,
And what did he find - but Teddy's football.

Grinning, he slid down the ladder with speed.

"Who was it," he winked, "did this terrible deed?"

"It was me!" said Teddy hanging his head,

As he shuffled his feet and went terribly red.

"Never mind," said mother, "there's no harm done.
   We'll clear up the mess, then have lunch in the sun."
The fire crew stayed and helped put things right,
   And everyone worked up a huge appetite.

It was just like a party, the bears had such fun.
But Teddy felt sorry for what he had done.
"Cheer up," laughed the fire crew. "Climb up inside.
Come and visit the station - we'll give you a ride!"
Teddy's frowns turned to smiles when the journey began.
"Do you think, for today, I could be a fireman?"

At the station the fire chief shouted "Hello!
    Come and look round, there's a lot you should know.
When you join the fire crew you wear special suits,
    Blue tunic with belt and a helmet and boots."

How smart all four looked in their fireman's clothes.
    Said Teddy, "Let's help them and unroll the hose."

Now the fire crew were testing equipment that day,
And all the Teddies just happened to be in the way.
The engine pumped water out in a jet,
Straight onto the Teddies - who got rather wet!

Teddy then asked the fire crew, "What do you do
To reach the top storey on a rescue?"
"We've no problem at all, to reach we're quite able
With our longest ladder. It's called a turntable!"

Said the fire chief, "We're having a practise today,
We would like volunteers to help right away,
To climb to the top of the building and shout,
So the crews can take part in a full scale turn out!"

All the Teddies agreed
they could come to no harm.
And off went the fire chief
to sound the alarm.
CLANG went the bell,
the crews rushed to the fire,
The turntable ladder
went higher and higher.

"Help, help!" yelled the Teddies. "Save us, please do!"
    "Hang on!" Fireman Bear called. "I've almost
    reached you."
He grabbed hold of Teddy and held him so tight.
    "Be careful, don't drop me!" gasped Teddy in fright.

But Teddy was carried down
quite safe and sound.
What a relief it was
when he reached the ground.
Back up the ladder
went the fire bear, so brave,
There were three more Teddies
he still had to save.

When he carried them down everyone gave three cheers
For the fire crew and the four brave volunteers.

Back in the station the crew took a break,
While waiting for fires - they often had cake!

"When you want to go home, we will give you a ride.
    If you want to save time, down the pole you must slide.
For a real fire bear it's the only way,
    And you four have been proper Fire Bears today!"